I'm Princess **Sofia** and I am so excited! Today we are playing croquet, while waiting for the **Enchanted Feast** to begin.

Baileywick arrives and tells
us that we have an unexpected visitor.

Baileywick presents Sascha the sorceress!
"I've come to pay my respects to the great
King Roland," the sorceress says.

She conjures up a
new sceptre
for Dad and some
flowers for Mum ...

**pretty
bracelets**
for Amber ...

and **shiny** new
boots for James!

Cedric arrives and introduces himself to Sascha.
"The Cedric the sorcerer?" she asks.
"It's an honour!"
Cedric blushes.

Mum and Dad invite Sascha
to the **Enchanted Feast**.
Everyone seems **SO** excited about
Sascha, but something just
doesn't seem right about her.

So I go to visit Cedric.
"I have a bad feeling around Sascha," I tell him.
"Since you're a sorcerer, too, I thought
you might know if she's up to something."

But Cedric just tells me
to stop worrying. He thinks
Sascha's great.

Then he shows me the trick he's planning for the feast. With a flick of his **wand**, he fills the whole room with mirrors.

But these aren't just any mirrors –
they're Morpho-Mirrors. "Wow! I look like
a totally different person in each one!" I say.

Finally the Enchanted Feast begins,
with guests from all over the kingdom.

Cedric makes a grand entrance
and gets ready for his trick.
He raises his wand....

Poof!

The Morpho-Mirrors appear.
But then something goes wrong!
The mirrors **trap** Cedric,
bouncing him like a ball from
one mirror to the next!

Nobody knows what to do – except Sascha. With one wave of her wand, she makes the mirrors **disappear**.

Then Sascha conjures up the most **amazing** food you've ever seen! Talk about an **enchanted feast!**

Everyone claps
Sascha the sorceress.
Well, everyone except Cedric,
who slips quietly out of the room.
"Cedric, wait!" I call, running after him.

But Cedric disappears into his tower.
Poor Cedric. I feel sorry for him.
Clover hops up and asks me what's wrong.

"Everyone thinks the
new sorceress is great," I tell him.

"But **something** about her just doesn't seem right."

Then my **amulet** starts to **glow!**

And Snow White appears!
She sits down and begins to tell me
a story. "Once an old woman gave
me a poisoned apple, but she was really
my wicked stepmother in disguise."

Snow White takes my hand.
"Sofia, people aren't always who they
pretend to be. If you have a bad feeling
about someone, you should trust
that feeling, no matter what."

Now I know what to do.
I've got to warn Mum and Dad about Sascha!

But when I reach the dining hall, Sascha is outside and vines are blocking the doors.

Suddenly ...

she transforms!

Now I know why she seemed so familiar. "Miss Nettle!" I cry.

Miss Nettle is a very bad **fairy**. Once she tried to steal a spell book from the good fairies, but I stopped her. "What are you doing here?" I ask.

Miss Nettle arrives at the Great Hall.

"You want the amulet?" I say.

"Come and get it!"

Miss Nettle flings a spell at me – at least, she thinks it's me. But it's really a mirror – so the spell bounces back and traps the bad fairy with her own magic!

But **Miss Nettle** escapes from the trap.

"You haven't seen the last of me!" she cries as she flies through the window.

Whew!
Now that she's gone,
we can all just have fun
with Cedric's **amazing**
Morpho-Mirrors!

I really hope Miss Nettle
never comes back. But if she does,
I'll be ready – thanks to the advice from my
new friend,
Snow White.

The
End